W9-ASL-853

DISCARD

HORRIBLE HARRY
MOVES UP TO
THIRD GRADE

BY SUZY KLINE
Pictures by Frank Remkiewicz

Viking

Special thanks to my editor, Cathy Hennessy, for her help with this manuscript; and to my husband, Rufus, for his sense of humor; and to my wonderful third-graders, who went with me to the Old New-Gate Prison and Copper Mine in East Granby, Connecticut.

VIKING
Published by the Penguin Group
Penguin Putnam Books for Young Readers, 345 Hudson Street,
New York, New York 10014, U.S.A.
Penguin Books Ltd, 27 Wrights Lane, London W8 5TZ, England
Penguin Books Australia Ltd, Ringwood, Victoria, Australia
Penguin Books Canada Ltd, 10 Alcorn Avenue, Toronto, Ontario, Canada M4V 3B2
Penguin Books (N.Z.) Ltd, 182–190 Wairau Road, Auckland 10, New Zealand

Penguin Books Ltd, Registered Offices: Harmondsworth, Middlesex, England

First published in 1998 by Viking, a member of Penguin Putnam Books for Young Readers.

7 9 10 8 6

Text copyright © Suzy Kline, 1998
Illustrations copyright © Frank Remkiewicz, 1998
All rights reserved

LIBRARY OF CONGRESS CATALOGING-IN-PUBLICATION DATA
Kline, Suzy.
Horrible Harry moves up to third grade / by Suzy Kline ; pictures
by Frank Remkiewicz.   p.   cm.
Summary: Horrible Harry and friends start off third grade with a
new room and a field trip to an old copper mine to study rocks.
ISBN 0-670-87873-1
[1. Schools—Fiction. 2. School field trips—Fiction.]
I. Remkiewicz, Frank, ill. II. Title.
PZ7.K6797Hp 1998 [Fic]—dc21 98–13098 CIP AC

Printed in U.S.A.   Set in New Century Schoolbook

Dedicated with love to my daughter Emily and my son-in-law Victor Hurtuk, who had their beautiful wedding in an old stone church in Connecticut, August 2, 1997.

Contents

Are We on Mars?

I couldn't wait for third grade in Room 2B.

Same class.

Same teacher.

Same room.

And most important . . . Harry and I would be *together* for another school year. Safe and sound.

Boy, was I wrong!

On the first day of school, Harry and I went walking down the hall.

"Ready for third grade, Doug?" he asked.

"I'm ready," I said.

We slapped each other five.

When we got to Room 2B, we stopped dead in our tracks. A tall man with green eyes and a bald head greeted us. "Welcome to school, boys!"

"You're *not* Miss Mackle," Harry said. "This is Miss Mackle's room!"

"No. I'm Mr. Moulder. I'm teaching second grade. This is my room now."

Harry stepped inside and looked around. "Are you hiding her somewhere?"

Mr. Moulder scratched his shiny head. "Hiding who?"

Harry and I exchanged looks. What was going on? Were we in the right school?

We ran outside the building to double-check. There it was in cement just above the door:

SOUTH SCHOOL
FOUNDED IN 1901

"This is crazy," I said.

"This is weird," Harry said. "We're supposed to have Miss Mackle for third grade. *Where is she?*"

We walked back into the building.

"Let's go to the office," I suggested.

When we got there, we saw a huge bouquet of flowers. Harry read the little note speared on the plastic fork:

CONGRATULATIONS, MRS. CARPENTER!

We looked at the lady sitting at the secretary's desk. She had her back to us. She was typing something on her computer.

"That's not Miss Foxworth," Harry said. "Miss Foxworth doesn't have blonde hair."

"Let's go ask Mrs. Chan, our old kindergarten teacher," I said.

We dashed down the hall.

"Can I help you boys?" asked a young woman who looked like Snow White. "I'm Miss Zaharek, the kindergarten teacher."

"AAAAHHHHHHH!" we screamed.

We started pounding our hands on the wall poster, "ALL I REALLY NEED TO KNOW I LEARNED IN KINDERGARTEN."

Finally, the principal showed up.

When we spotted his curly hair and

mustache, we cheered, *"Mr. Cardini!"*

"Well, hello, Harry and Doug. You boys lost?"

"Yeah!" Harry said with his fist in the air. "It feels like we're on Mars!"

Mr. Cardini laughed as he twirled his mustache. "I think you two are looking for your third-grade room. That's upstairs. Didn't you read the number on your old report card?"

Harry and I shrugged.

"Take a left at the top of the stairs. Room 3B is the second room on the right side of the hall."

Harry and I took off like two road-runners. We zoomed up the stairs in seconds, then took a left and counted two rooms down on the right side.

"This room must be Mars," Harry said. "Look at these boulders stacked outside the door."

"Just a minute," I said. "These aren't real rocks. They're grocery bags from Park and Shop crunched up and sprayed brown."

Harry smelled the rocks and saw the faint lettering through the paint. "Yeah. They're phony."

Slowly, we passed through the boulder archway. When we stepped inside, we were greeted by a big sign on the bulletin board. It said, THIRD GRADE ROCKS. There were lots of rocks on the display table, but we didn't go over and look at them. We just noticed the class.

"Hi, Harry! Hi, Doug!" everyone

shouted. There were Song Lee, Mary, Sidney, Ida, Dexter . . .

. . . and *Miss Mackle*!

Harry ran over and gave her a big hug.

I waved.

I was just as glad to see her, though.

"Welcome to third grade, boys. I can't wait to hear about your summer."

"Forget summer. What's going on here?" I asked.

"Yeah," Harry replied. "Who's that bald guy in Room 2B. And where are Miss Foxworth and Mrs. Chan?"

Miss Mackle smiled. "Every summer brings some changes. As you know, we moved upstairs. And South School just hired two new teachers. Mr. Moulder for second grade, and Miss Zaharek in kindergarten. Mrs. Chan retired."

"What happened to Miss Foxworth? Did she fall off a cliff or something?"

"No, Harry," Miss Mackle said. "She got married over the summer and changed her name. Now she's Mrs. Carpenter."

"She looks different," I said.

"She changed her hair," Miss Mackle said. "She's a blonde now."

"Ooooooh," we replied.

When the bell rang, Harry and I found our seats. They had our names on them. Mine was by the window. Harry's was next to the pencil sharpener and wastepaper basket. He seemed to like that. He gave me the thumbs-up sign.

I wasn't so sure, so I just nodded.

Was *everything* going to change in third grade?

Two Things in Third Grade That *Didn't* Change

The first thing I did when I sat down was look out the window. Everything looked so different from the second floor. Last year, I could see the school Dumpster, lawns, and cars on the street. Now there were just clouds and the sky.

"Look!" Harry blurted out from across the room. "There goes Lifestar, the helicopter. I bet it's taking a bloody person to the hospital."

Mary made a face. "I was hoping *you* might change over the summer, Harry. But you haven't," she groaned. "You're still gross."

I smiled.

At least that was *one thing* I could count on.

Ida raised her hand. "Where's the monitor chart, Miss Mackle?"

"Up here, *in cursive*," she said, pointing to the front bulletin board.

It looked like Greek to me. I tried reading it:

Third Grade Employment

Class Leaders	Harry and Sidney
Zookeeper	Mary
Forester	Song Lee
Custodian	Dexter
Equipment Manager	Doug
Courier	Ida

I couldn't even read the job I had.

The rest of the kids' names were in the envelope at the bottom. I couldn't read the words on that either:

Temporarily Unemployed

"Welcome to third grade, boys and girls," Miss Mackle said. "I am so excited that we looped. Here we are for a second year together! I hope you all got my postcard asking you to bring a summer memento to class."

Everyone nodded.

Even Harry.

Harry did his homework? Now I knew I was on another planet!

"Before we have our morning conversation about our summer, let's have our class leaders start the pledge."

Harry and Sidney each carried a

small flag to the front of the room. I knew why Miss Mackle put *them* together. They have a tough time getting along. Sidney does something stupid and then Harry gets revenge.

I wondered if that would change, too?

After the pledge and "The Star-Spangled Banner," we all sat down at our desks. "Now," Miss Mackle said, "let's share our summer experiences. Song Lee, will you begin?"

Song Lee opened the brown bag on her lap.

Everyone leaned forward to see what was inside.

"My aunt visited us from Korea. When we took a walk, I found this."

We watched Song Lee hold up a jar that had something golden inside. It looked like an egg wrapped in silk.

"Aunt Sun Yee and I found this under a fence post. It is a spider egg sac. In the spring, it will hatch into many spiders just like Charlotte's magnum opus."

Miss Mackle sighed. "Ohhhh . . ."

I could tell the teacher loved Song Lee's memento. She put her hand over her heart.

"Can I go next?" Sidney blurted out. "I've got a momento, too."

"Memento," Mary corrected. "No, you

can't go next. I have a question for
Song Lee. What did you put on top of
your jar?"

Song Lee giggled. "Aunt Sun Yee's
pantyhose. We cut up an old pair."

When everyone laughed, I thought about Song Lee. She spoke English so well now.

"Can we keep the egg sac in the classroom?" Dexter asked.

"Yes," Song Lee replied. After we all watched her set the jar gently on the science table, we raised our hands again.

"Go ahead, Sidney," Miss Mackle said.

"Finally," Sidney groaned.

Then he started unwrapping something in aluminum foil. "My stepdad and I did a lot of barbecuing this summer, so I brought this as a souvenir."

We watched Sidney hold up a burnt wiener.

"It got left on the grill." Sidney cackled.

A lot of people laughed, but Harry and

I didn't. We thought it was dumb. Who would bring something like that to class?

Sidney LaFleur.

I went next.

"I brought rocks," I said. "I got them at the Old New-Gate Prison and Copper Mine in East Granby. They're real copper. And this is an old Granby copper coin."

When I held the stuff up, everyone oooohed and aaahhed.

"Gee, Doug," Miss Mackle said, writing something down on her clipboard. "That would be a great place to visit, since we're studying rocks in science! Maybe I could arrange a class field trip to that mine."

"Yeah!" everyone said.

Oh boy, I thought secretly. That's

what I get for leaving one small part out of my story. I never went *down* into that mine. I was too chicken. Two days before my family went to Old New-Gate Prison and Copper Mine, Harry and I had watched the movie *Tom Sawyer.* It was great except for one awful part where Tom and Becky get lost in the mine, and Injun Joe falls down the hole in a cave. I made up my mind then, I would *never* go under-ground.

Please, God, I prayed. Don't let us go on a class field trip to *that mine.*

"Okay," Harry said. "My turn." And he held up a picture of himself in that scary elevator ride, THE DROP OF DOOM, at Mountainside Park. "I wasn't afraid at all," he bragged. "It was a piece of cake."

That made Song Lee and me roll our eyes.

We knew better.

Sidney cracked up. "Yeah. Tell me more, Old Yeller! Tell the truth! Tell 'em you had a HUGE case of the heebie-jeebies!"

When Harry held up a fist, I knew what he was thinking. Revenge.

That was the second thing that didn't change in third grade.

I just worried what Harry might do.

A Deadly Event

Things took a nosedive the next day when Harry brought something to school in a shoe box.

The box had cellophane on top so you could look inside. All we could see, though, was dirt, some grass, a rock, a plastic lid, and a toilet-paper tube.

"Oh no," Ida groaned. "Does that box have a snake in it like the first day in second grade?"

"Nope." Harry grinned.

"Something better," he said. "My mom

read me *Charlotte's Web* this summer, and I got interested in spiders."

Miss Mackle beamed. "I remember when I read that book to you last year."

"Yeah," Harry said. "I will never forget our invasion of the cobwebs. Well, there's a *real* spider and cobweb in this box, and I have to get him some fresh water."

Sidney cringed.

We watched Harry open up the trapdoor on the side of the box, pull out a small lid, and take it over to the classroom sink to fill it with water. When he returned, he put it carefully back inside.

"Now I'll close the trapdoor so Charles can't get out."

"Charles?" Sidney scoffed. "You gave your spider a name?"

"Of course," Harry snapped. "He's

my pet spider. I found him in my bathtub a week ago."

"I didn't know spiders took baths,"
Sidney said.

"They don't," Harry groaned. "He
was just thirsty. A bathtub is a good
place to find some water."

"What kind of spider is he?" Miss
Mackle asked.

"Just an ordinary one with eight legs and eight eyeballs," Harry said. "He has everything he needs in this spider house. I just have to feed him a fly now and then."

"I hate spiders," Sidney said. "They're bloodsuckers."

Mary put her hands on her hips. "Spiders have to eat, too! Charlotte explained all of that."

"I think I'll make a spider house for my egg sac after school," Song Lee said.

"I'll help you," Mary replied.

Harry and I started pulling books about spiders out of the library corner.

Mary and Song Lee got their science notebooks and started drawing pictures of Charles.

Dexter and Ida made a spider board game about *Charlotte's Web* with pink chance cards.

"What were the names of Charlotte's three grandchildren?" Dexter said as he wrote the question down. "Name them and you advance three spaces."

And then at 10:07 it happened.

When everyone was busy.

Harry was over by the windows trapping a fly for Charles's meal.

"*Auuuuuuuugh!*" Sidney screamed. "The spider just crawled out the trapdoor. He's gonna get me!"

Harry put down his flyswatter and raced over.

But not in time.

Sidney took one of my copper rocks and smashed the spider.

Blam!

"*You killed C h a r l e s !*" Harry yelled.

Miss Mackle rushed over.

Everyone made a circle around the science table.

"He was trying to escape," Sidney pleaded. "He was going to bite me. I did what I had to do."

No one said anything.

Slowly Harry put up two fists.

Uh-oh, I thought. Now he's thinking Double Revenge.

Miss Mackle called us over to the braided rug in the library corner. "Please sit down, boys and girls," she said.

We did.

"Spiders are nature's best friends. They eat harmful insects. They help plants grow. We don't have to be afraid of them."

Mary sneered. "*Sidney's* the only one afraid of spiders."

Everyone stared at Sidney.

"So?" he said. "They can kill you."

Miss Mackle drew something on her

clipboard. "There are two spiders that are deadly. Both have special markings. The black widow has . . ."

". . . a red hourglass on its abdomen," Harry interrupted.

"Yes. And the other has a violin marking on its back. That's the brown recluse."

Everyone studied the teacher's drawings.

"But most spiders are harmless."

Sidney made a face. "They're not my best friends." Then he paused. "I am . . . sorry . . . about Charlie."

"His name was *Charles*," Harry snapped.

"Well, I think we should have a moment of silence for Harry's dead pet," Mary suggested.

"That sounds like a good idea," the teacher replied.

So we did. We bowed our heads and closed our eyes and thought about Charles. Then Miss Mackle took us downstairs for a drink and a run in the sun. I think she wanted us to air out our brains.

When we came back to the room, Sidney started looking around for something. "Hey," he blurted out, "someone stole my burnt wiener!"

Things Get Rocky

The next week, things got a lot rockier between Harry and Sidney. When we were getting off the bus, Harry said, "Hey, Sid, how would you like to see me eat rocks for breakfast?"

"Huh?" Sidney peeked in the bag of rocks Harry was carrying. There was mica and pyrite and granite and quartz.

"How'd you like to see me eat rocks," Harry repeated.

Sidney's eyes bulged. "I'd love to see you do that."

"Well, it's going to cost you something," Harry said.

"You can't have my milk money," Sidney warned.

"I don't want your milk money," Harry replied. "I want something else."

"What?"

"To see if you can run around the playground four times and get to our room before the bell rings."

"That's it?"

Harry nodded. "I'll be standing by the window counting to make sure you run each lap."

Mary and Song Lee and Ida took a step back. "You're eating rocks for breakfast?" they said.

"If Sidney does his part of the bargain," Harry said.

"You're lookin' at the roadrunner,"
Sidney said. "See you in the room when
you eat . . . rocks!"

And he took off!

Harry and I dashed upstairs and
peered out the classroom window.
There was Sidney racing around the
playground. Each time he ran a lap,
Harry held a finger up.

Every now and then, Sidney would
look up to see if Harry was watching.

When Harry held up three fingers, I looked at the clock. Five minutes to go!

Sidney was slowing down now. Finally he finished the fourth lap.

Just as he got in the room and plopped down in his seat, the bell rang.

"I . . . I . . . made . . . it," Sidney gasped. His hands were touching the floor. "Now . . . it's . . . it's . . . time for . . . your . . . part of . . . the bargain."

Harry opened up his backpack and reached for a napkin. He tucked it inside his shirt.

Song Lee and Mary looked worried when he set the bag of heavy rocks on his desk.

"Here I go!" he said. Then he reached into his backpack and pulled out a box of salt and shook some out on his tongue. "Mmmmm, poor man's potato chips."

Sidney sat up. "What are you doing? You're not eating rocks. You're eating salt."

"That's what salt is, Sid. Rocks." Harry leaned back in his chair just enough so he wouldn't fall, and sprinkled some more salt in his mouth. "Deeeeelicous!"

Sidney crossed his arms. "I ran myself ragged to see you eat salt?"

"Yup," Harry said, licking his lips.

Mary and Ida smiled. Song Lee giggled. I just put two thumbs up. Sid had it coming for killing Harry's spider.

I was actually enjoying third grade, until Miss Mackle made that dreaded announcement.

Murder in the Mine

The next morning Miss Mackle said, "Boys and girls, we are going to the Old New-Gate Prison and Copper Mine September thirtieth!"

When everyone cheered, I motioned to Harry to meet me at the pencil sharpener. I had to talk with him.

Harry broke his pencil on the side of the desk, then joined me.

"What's up?" he asked.

"Remember how you were kind of

scared to ride the elevator in the Drop of Doom?"

Harry paused. He never liked admitting he was afraid of anything.

"Yeah . . ." he barely whispered.

"Well, I never went down into that copper mine. I was . . . afraid." It was hard for me to say it, too.

Harry flashed his white teeth. "Hey, Doug, you can do it. If I could do the Doom ride, you can walk through a mine. Pretend you're a spider. They love cool, dark places."

"Thanks, Harry," I groaned.

After I sharpened my pencil, I added, "You'll stick close by?"

"Like Elmer's glue," he whispered.

September thirtieth came too soon.

Song Lee and Ida and Mary sat in front of Harry and me on the bus. The girls played hangman. Their first word had eight letters.

PRISONER

I sure felt like one sitting next to Harry. I was trapped, and there was no getting out of it.

Harry could tell I was getting nervous. My knees were shaking. He opened his backpack. "Try not to think about it. Think about other things, like . . ."

Then Harry pulled out something wrapped in aluminum foil. "Remember this?"

I watched Harry unwrap it.

"Sidney's burnt wiener!" I said.

"Shhhh!" Harry put a finger to his mouth. "He's sitting across the aisle. It's a secret. Ol' Sid doesn't know I have it."

"What are *you* doing with it?"

"I'm not sure. I might just keep it

until it becomes a fossil."

"A wiener fossil?" When I laughed, my knees stopped shaking.

"Sure. Or . . . it might come in handy sometime for something else."

Harry.

He was a piece of work.

I sure was glad he was my partner. He made me forget about things when we were on the bus.

An hour later, we got to the mine. We got off the bus and walked over to the little museum shop. It was fun to crunch through all the autumn leaves. The trees were red, orange, yellow, and brown. It was a beautiful sunny day, I kept telling myself.

The inside of the museum was small. There were all kinds of books for sale, some rocks, and Granby copper coins. There were also soda and candy machines, but Miss Mackle stood in front of them like a football guard. "Spend your money wisely," she said.

Sidney made a long face. He had his coins ready. "Man, that's no fair. I wanted to get a crunchy chocolate bar."

As soon as I spotted the boys' room, I ducked inside. I always have to go when I get nervous.

Later, when everyone had bags of souvenirs, a gray-haired man said, "Welcome, boys and girls, gather 'round. You are about to visit the first copper mine in the thirteen colonies. It also was our first state prison. Back in the 1700s, prisoners worked in the mine."

"What crimes did they commit?" Mary asked. She had her pencil and notebook and was taking notes.

"Most of them were horse thieves, counterfeiters, and burglars."

"What did the burglars steal?" Sidney asked.

"Well, in 1780, seven men broke into Captain Ebenezer Dayton's house and tied up his wife with a torn sheet."

"Where was Ebenezer?" Mary snapped.

"He was out of town."

Mary rolled her eyes.

"So, what happened?" Harry asked.

"Well, they kept her tied up in a chair for two hours while they ransacked the house. They took coats, cloaks, gowns, silk handkerchiefs, silver shoe buckles, a spyglass, two muskets, four halberds, and four hundred fifty pounds of gold, silver, and copper coins."

"What's a halberd?" Mary asked.

"It's a long-handled ax."

We followed the elderly man outside to a courtyard and brick wall. When he leaned over, he picked up some rocks. "Just about everywhere you look you can see copper rocks. If it has green on it, it's copper."

Mary bent down and pointed at something green. "This isn't copper," she said. "It's someone's half-eaten lime lollipop."

"Gross," Ida said. "There's a spider on it, too."

"Don't kill it," Harry said, looking at Sidney.

"Single file please," the guide said. "We're about to enter the mine."

"Oh boy," I said to Harry. "Here we go."

Harry walked right behind me. He was so close I could feel his warm breath on my neck. "Remember, Doug. You're a spider. You love the underground world."

"I'll try," I whispered. Slowly, I walked into the mine. The path ahead of me zigzagged down a sloping hill. The space seemed to get smaller and darker. I clung to the railing when there was one.

"Neato," Harry said. "This is cool."

The guide heard Harry. "Actually, it is fifty-two degrees all year round in this mine."

"Cool," Harry repeated.

I stopped walking and looked at my

arms. There were goose pimples on them!

"Keep moving," Harry said.

"I like the lanterns along the path into the mine," Mary said. "They're neat."

"Hey! Water is dripping on my head!" Ida said.

"It tickles!" Song Lee giggled.

The guide smiled. "There's water in the earth. We're inside the earth now."

Inside the earth?

I was really underground!

As the hike got darker and wetter, and the stone ceiling got lower and lower, I got more afraid. I wasn't going to tell anyone, though. I just bent over as I walked, and stayed closer to Harry.

Ten minutes later, it seemed like we were miles inside the earth. My heart was beating like one of those huge gongs.

Song Lee took a picture. "I love rocks," she said. "Maybe I'll be a miner when I grow up."

Not me, I thought. What if some boulders fell and blocked our way back? What if I fell down a hole like Injun Joe?

Finally, I had to ask the question.

"How much longer are we going to stay down here?"

"About ten minutes," the guide said.

Ten minutes. That was ten times sixty seconds, which made six hundred seconds to go.

I started counting backward. "Six hundred, five hundred ninety-nine, five hundred ninety-eight . . ."

Sidney must have noticed I was nervous because he started teasing me about it. "Got a case of the heebie-jeebies like *Harry* did on that Drop of Doom ride last summer?"

Harry raised a fist.

When Sidney laughed, I could hear Harry growl.

"You can see over here, there is a large deposit of copper," the guide said, as he shone his flashlight in the corner.

Sidney turned around and whispered,

"It's really the green boogeyman."

Suddenly, I got mad. I never believed boogeyman stories. Sidney wasn't going to frighten me! Now I was more determined than ever to pretend I was not afraid. I kept on counting, only this time I didn't say it out loud.

Harry gave Sidney a final warning. "You'd better stop fooling around, Sid the Squid."

After we turned and entered a small empty room, the guide asked everyone to sit down for a while and rest. His voice echoed off the stone walls.

"I have a ghost story to tell you," he said.

I grabbed Harry's ankle and held on to it tightly.

"There once was a prisoner named Abel Starkey who saved one hundred dollars."

"What was he in for?" Mary asked.

"Counterfeiting money. He was serving a twenty-year sentence."

The guide continued the story. *"Starkey offered the cash to a guard if he helped him escape. The guard agreed because he wanted the money. He told Starkey about a path in the mine that was rarely used. It was behind a locked metal door. It led to an underground well that had an old rope used for pulling buckets. The guard said Starkey could use it to climb to freedom.*

"What the guard didn't tell Starkey was that the rope was frayed in the middle. The guard didn't really want Starkey to escape. It was too risky. What if Starkey got caught? the guard thought. What if he told on him?

"The night of the escape, when everyone was sleeping in the mine, Starkey sneaked down the path to the old metal

door. Yes! The guard had left it unlocked. Starkey opened it and raced to the well. When he got there, he climbed onto the rope and pulled himself up, up, up.

"When he got halfway, the rope snapped, and he fell to his death. Legend has it that Starkey's ghost still roams the mine today searching for a way out."

Sidney closed his eyes and groped around with his hands.

"Oooooooouch!" Harry said. "You hit my head."

"I am Starkey's ghost walking through the mine . . ."

"Cut it out, Sid," Harry growled. He knew I was in bad shape.

When Sidney kept it up, Harry unbuckled his backpack and took something out. It was too dark to see what.

Then Harry stood up and tapped

Sidney on the shoulder with his finger.

"What?" Sidney said.

Harry didn't answer. He just kept tapping Sidney's shoulder.

"Stop tapping me!"

When Harry didn't stop, Sidney grabbed Harry's finger and pulled on it.

"Auugh!" Sidney screamed. "I pulled Harry's finger off!"

"AUUGH!" the class yelled. We could tell Sidney was holding on to something and flopping it in the air.

When the guide shone his flashlight

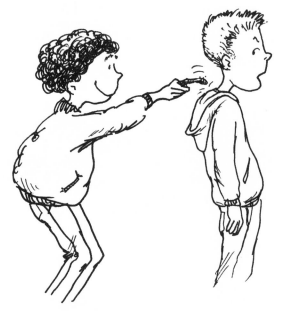

on Sidney's hand, we all groaned. *"The burnt wiener!"*

"So *you were the one who stole it!"* Sid said, glaring at Harry.

"I borrowed it," he said. "And now I'm returning it to you."

Everybody started cracking up, including me. It felt good to laugh in the middle of that dark, wet mine. It also felt good when we started walking back, and when I first spotted light at the top of the mine entrance.

As soon as I got outside, I lay down on the ground and kissed the grass. "Ahhhhh," I said. "Sweet earth, beautiful sky, delicious dirt."

Harry punched me in the arm.

"You did it, Spido."

I punched Harry back in the arm. "Yeah, I did, didn't I?"

Miss Mackle tapped my head as she made a quick count of our class.

Suddenly, she exclaimed, *"We're missing one student!"*

Sidney Disappears!

The chaperones counted heads again.

"There's twenty, not twenty-one," Miss Mackle said. "Who's missing?"

Harry and I knew right away. "Sidney," we said.

"*Sidney! Sidney!*" everyone called.

The guide and two of the chaperones went back into the mine.

Miss Mackle looked really scared as she paced back and forth. I had never seen her look like that before. "Keep calling his name," she ordered.

"Sidney! Sidney!"

The guide came back with the chaperones. "He's not in the mine. The pathway isn't that wide. We would have seen him."

"Maybe he fell down a hole," Mary said.

Mary.

She was always the voice of doom.

Harry started to feel a little guilty. "Maybe I shouldn't have done that finger trick with the wiener."

Song Lee and Mary ran with a chaperone to check the museum.

When they came back, they were shaking their heads.

"He wasn't there."

Miss Mackle looked like she was going to cry. *"Where is he?"*

"He's . . . not on . . . the bus," another

chaperone reported. She was out of breath.

"Oh no." When Miss Mackle bowed her head, everyone knew she was praying.

Then, suddenly, out of nowhere, Sidney appeared! He strolled across the courtyard, crunching the fall leaves.

When he got closer, I noticed there was chocolate smeared in the corners of his mouth.

Everyone was cheering, even Harry.

Miss Mackle put two hands over her heart.

"Sidney!" she gasped.

"What's everyone so upset about? I just had to go to the can. When everyone started laughing about that finger story, I did, too. Then nature called and I ran out of the mine. Pronto!"

57

I made a face. I didn't think that was the full story, but I didn't say anything.

Harry was the first to give Sidney a hug. "I'm sure glad you're not dead like that Starkey guy."

"Thanks, Harry," Sidney replied. "That's the first compliment I ever got from you."

And he hugged him back.

Miss Mackle hugged Sidney too, but then she looked him in the eye and firmly said, "Don't you ever leave the group again without permission."

The beginning of third grade was sure full of surprises and changes, but the ones on our field trip were the biggest and the best.

Harry and Sidney made up.

And I made it out of that mine.